F.R.O.G

Fully Rely On God

BY JERRILYN ASH

xulon PRESS

This book is lovingly dedicated to

Mrs. Nancy Osborn,

Sunday School Teacher

Extraordinaire!

#1 FROG SONG

Once there was
A little green frog
Who liked to sit
On an old, mossy log.
    He'd sing praises to God
    Til by and by,
    His long pink tongue
    Would snatch up a fly.

    And he'd sing:

    His song was heard
    Throughout the bog
    Always the same,
    "FULLY RELY ON GOD!"

He swam everyday
In a small, cool pond--
With family and friends
Of whom he was fond.
    He'd bask on the leaf
    Of a lily pad
    Sharing some time
    With his mom and dad,

And he'd sing.

His song was heard
Throughout the bog
Always the same,
"FULLY RELY ON GOD!"

Danger lurked,
But he didn't quake.
He prayed for protection
From every snake
Who slithered about
Looking for a meal,
And wondering why
Frogs had no appeal.

Near the old log
Was a big yellow cat
Who'd sneak through the grass
To where the frog sat.
His eyes would squint,
His tail would twitch,
He'd leap for the frog
Who'd escape in a ditch.

So, when you get nervous
And the road looks too rough,
Remember this frog,
And why he could stay tough.
Don't rely on your wits--
They won't be enough
To keep you safe
From all the bad stuff.

Sing like the frog
At the top of your voice;
Ask God for guidance
In every choice.

His song was heard
Throughout the bog
Always the same,
"FULLY RELY ON GOD!"

#2 HOME

The pond in the park
Was a great feature
Providing a home
For many a creature.

One spring, there appeared
Amidst the watery grass
A strange looking jelly
All in a mass.

There were dark spots in the center
Of each soft, jellied cell.
That in time became tadpoles
With legs and tails-do tell!

But these frog eggs and tadpoles
Have great appeal
To fish and big birds-
They make a good meal.

So, many of the tadpoles
Just never grew
Into proper frogs -
Only a few.

But one frog who survived
Was special and wise.
He had love in his heart
Of quite a large size.

He was always polite
And made the choice
Of singing God's praises
At the top of his voice!

His song was heard
Throughout the bog
Always the same:
"FULLY RELY ON GOD!"

Fully Rely On God.

The first letter of each word
Makes an acronym
Spelling 'FROG'
Yes, that's him.

He had great adventures
For a frog, that is.
He enjoyed every day
And became a whiz

At understanding things
Where he was residing,
Being careful to avoid
Bad things from colliding.

He followed the rules
And became a great frog
Who watched over the pond
From an old, mossy log.

So, be like the frog,
Have love in your heart.
Keep God first in your life,
Become a part

Of the chorus of praise
Who sing with a nod
Knowing they're loved:
"FULLY RELY ON GOD!"

#3 RUNAWAY FROG, RESCUED

Could be tragic,
Always a pity
To see a frog
Lost in the city.

Huddled under
A small scrap of trash,
If he gets stepped on
He becomes hash.

Things weren't going
Quite right back home.
Frog got irate
And decided to roam.

He hopped through the park
With spite in his heart,
Forgetting what he knew
About being a part.

Of God's great creation
His place in the bog,
And safety and comfort
On an old mossy log.

Now, he is sorry,
But what to do?
Checking his options
He had but a few.

Recalling his song
And all that it meant,
He opened his mouth
And to Heaven sent

His song, which was known
All through the bog;
Always the same:
"FULLY RELY ON GOD!"

All of a sudden,
Rain started to fall
Folks ran for shelter
And into the mall!

Traffic stopped;
Drivers couldn't see
And Frog recognized
His chance to flee.

He hopped off the sidewalk
Across the street, and then--
Went straight to the park
Rejoicing again!

His hops became leaps--
He sped really fast.
In just a few minutes,
He was home--at last.

He never shared
Tales of his flight,
But knew in his heart
The peril of fright.

Clinging to the truth
And doing your best,
Makes you a winner
As you pass every test!

There's a lilt to his voice,
Back in the bog,
As he sings out his message:
"FULLY RELY ON GOD!"

#4 CONTENTMENT

Diving and swimming
Eating some bugs
Hopping and leaping
Sharing wet hugs.

These are the things
Frogs usually do
If they live in a pond
 With a nice park view.

They learn a lot
From those strolling by
Who talk of their lives,
And sometimes cry.

Frog often pondered
The mystery
Of people's ambitions,
Striving to be

What they were not,
Never giving it rest,
N   nizing
G   best.

14

People demand changes
Always grasping for more
Weighing evidence -
Who's rich? Who's poor?

A frog's life is simpler
And way lots more fun.
Snatch a bug now and then
Bask in the sun.

Waking each morning
Smiling at things,
Secure that the day
Is under God's wings.

They speak softly and kindly
Respectful of all.
They don't measure worth
By who's short? Who's tall?

Envy is useless
It doesn't produce.
Enjoy what you have
Keep yourself loose.

That's Frog's advice
And who could know better
Than one who beats the heat
By just getting wetter?

So, sing when you want to
Or croak like this frog
But always remember:
"FULLY RELY ON GOD!"

SCRIPTURAL REFERENCES

Studying God's Word
Is a fun thing to do,
You search out the verse
Following each clue.

You'll be assured
Of God's watchful care,
And be encouraged
To learn and to share.

You can carry Frog's music
On your Ipod
Make it your song:
"FULLY RELY ON GOD!"

The Frog's Favorite Bible Verse

- James 5: 13 "Is any one of you troubled? He should pray.
Is anyone happy? He should sing!" (NIV)

Additional Verses for Study

- John 3: 16

- John 14: 1

- Psalm 46: 1-3

- Psalm 56: 3

- Philippians 4: 11-13

CPSIA information can be obtained
at www.ICGtesting.com
Printed in the USA
LVHW061548280721
693944LV00007B/332

9 781498 442367